R.L. STINE

GIVE YOURSELF

Goosebumps®

SPECIAL EDITION #7
POWER PLAY:

TRICK OR . . . TRAPPED!

AN
APPLE
PAPERBACK

SCHOLASTIC INC.
New York Toronto London Auckland Sydney
Mexico City New Delhi Hong Kong

A PARACHUTE PRESS BOOK

No part of this publication may be reproduced in whole or in part, or stored in a retrieval system, or transmitted in any form or by any means, electronic, mechanical, photocopying, recording, or otherwise, without written permission of the publisher. For information regarding permission, write to Scholastic Inc., Attention: Permissions Department, 555 Broadway, New York, NY 10012.

ISBN 0-590-99393-3

Copyright © 1999 by Parachute Press, Inc. All rights reserved. Published by Scholastic Inc. APPLE PAPERBACKS, SCHOLASTIC, and associated logos are trademarks and/or registered trademarks of Scholastic Inc. GOOSEBUMPS is a registered trademark of Parachute Press, Inc.

12 11 10 9 8 7 6 5 4 3 2 1   9/9 0 1 2 3 4/0

Printed in the U.S.A.   40

First Scholastic printing, October 1999

"Finally!" You breathe a sigh of relief. Your front door slams shut behind you.

You thought you'd never get out of there!

What an evening! First, your mother made you finish all your chores. Then, your dad ordered you to do your math homework. To top it off, your sister's white poodle bit you on the leg. Then, when you complained, your mom yelled at *you*!

But now you're running down your sidewalk carrying your trick-or-treat bag. In just a few hours it'll be filled to the brim with candy!

Halloween! you think with a grin. My kind of holiday!

You catch your reflection in the front windshield of your dad's car. Yes! Your vampire costume looks good.

"I have come to suck your blood!" you shout. Then you tear off to meet your three best buddies on Pearl Street. This is going to be your most awesome Halloween ever!

Run on to PAGE 2.

You take a shortcut that leads you onto a wide lane.

Directly in front of you, you see a wrought-iron gate. Behind it, in the distance, is an absolutely enormous white mansion. In front of the mansion — blocking any entrance to it — sit five homes in a row, each one a different color: red, blue, orange, yellow, and green. Weird. You've never noticed this place before.

"It's Sunshine Court!" someone says in your ear. You wheel around. Standing behind you is Nathan Rickles, the nerdiest, klutziest guy in your class. Just one look at him makes you remember the time his shorts caught on fire in the science lab. It takes all your concentration to keep from laughing.

"What's Sunshine Court?" you ask.

"Candy central!" Nathan exclaims, cleaning the glasses he wears over his zombie costume. "Trick-or-treating paradise! A caramel-coated jackpot!"

You sigh, remembering Nathan's tendency to repeat the same information ten different ways.

"Well, enjoy it," you say. "I have to meet some people."

But Nathan grabs you. "Not so fast!"

Stay with Nathan on PAGE 3.

Nathan holds a bag up to your nose. "Look what I got in there," he says. You peer inside the bag. Whoa! It's filled to the brim with candy!

"All that came from five houses?" you ask.

"Six, including the white mansion," Nathan replies. "You have to get to the white mansion. It's the best! The greatest! The —"

"Okay," you say. "I get the point." You stare through the heavy iron gates. Hmmm ... Your friends are waiting for you on Pearl Street — but how long could it take to visit five homes and a mansion?

"Here," Nathan says. "Take something to get you started." He places a Double-Chocolate-Triple-Caramel Delight in your bag!

"Wow, Nathan," you say. "That's my favorite! Thanks!"

"No problem," he replies. "Go on in — and don't forget the white mansion!"

Nathan runs off down the street.

You turn to the wrought-iron gate. Is it locked, you wonder? You push it. It swings open!

"Well," you say to yourself. "Candy, here I come!"

Hurry on to PAGE 4.

You sprint toward the houses.

CLANK!

You wheel around. The iron gates have shut behind you! You pull on them. Hey! They won't budge. Are they locked?

If they are, how will you ever get out of here? The iron fence circles the whole of Sunshine Court! For a second you're a little spooked. Everything is eerily still.

What was that? Did something move in the shadows?

You glance around. The grass here is perfectly mowed. Birds are singing in the trees. It looks like just the kind of neighborhood your parents would love to live in.

Stop being a dope, you scold yourself. There's nothing to be afraid of! The wind blew that gate shut. And someone in one of these houses will let you out. So get in there and trick-or-treat!

The cobblestone walk you're standing on splits into five directions, each leading to one of the five different-colored homes. Which one should you visit first?

To visit the red house, go to PAGE 100.
To visit the blue house, go to PAGE 9.
To visit the orange house, go to PAGE 63.
To visit the yellow house, go to PAGE 40.
To visit the green house, go to PAGE 120.

You reach the third floor. Before you is a game room.

It's as long as a basketball court and filled with pool tables, Ping-Pong tables, Skee Ball, and video games as far as the eye can see.

Then you notice something else. Just as Nathan promised, on the far side of the room is a set of bumper cars!

In any other situation you'd be in paradise. Too bad you're running for your life! Snap out of it, you think. You have to find a place to hide!

Behind the video games? No, not enough cover there.

How about under the pool table? Or in a bumper car?

Better make up your mind fast. . . .

The Thing is sure to be on your tail soon!

If you hide under the pool table, go to PAGE 32.
If you hide in a bumper car, go to PAGE 44.

You kick and claw. You scream at the top of your lungs. But the gorilla has you locked tight in his arms.

He carries you down a twisting hallway. You glance in the rooms to the left and right — and gasp!

In one room a group of mummies plays cards. In the next are two men playing Ping-Pong. But neither of them has a head!

Hillenthrobben notices the look of fear on your face. "Just some of my experiments," he explains.

Samson carries you into a giant laboratory and plops you down on an operating table.

Operating table? Are you about to become one of Hillenthrobben's experiments? "Let me go!" you cry.

But Samson simply ties you to the table.

"Finally!" Hillenthrobben cries. "The perfect child to use in my latest experiment!"

Oh, no! You can't even imagine what that means! You scream and try to kick. But you can't move your legs.

You're not entirely out of luck, though. Right next to your left hand is a lever. If you use it, maybe you can escape! You can either push it away, or pull it toward you.

If you push the lever away from you, go to PAGE 105.

If you pull the lever toward you, go to PAGE 107.

You grab the mask and try to cradle it in your palm. . . .

But the captain sees what you've done! You're caught.

"What's this?" he says, eyes wide.

The captain's green eyes narrow. He rips the gas mask from your hands. And steps toward you with the drill!

Please, you pray. Please, don't let this hurt!

WHHHHIIIRRRRR! The sound of the drill meets your ears.

Wait a second! This *doesn't* hurt! In fact, Billington fills your cavities with no pain whatsoever.

"All done," he tells you after a few minutes. "Your teeth are fine now but your gums need help. You've got to floss! And after every meal too!"

You nod vigorously. Right about now, you'd agree to almost anything to get free.

"Good!" Billington says, smiling again. "Well, you know the way out. Have fun!"

You tear out of the green house and stand in the middle of Sunshine Court. You have to get out of here!

And you think you see your ticket home. Rising up in front of you is the white mansion! Maybe there's someone in there who can help you get out of here!

Go to PAGE 108.

SWOOSH!

What's this? You're not falling anymore.

You feel yourself being lifted in the sky!

You open your eyes and gasp!

Yikes! A giant bird has your vampire cape in its beak. You're being carried toward the clouds!

You look down. You're so far up, the trees seem tiny. Your heart thuds in your chest.

This bird better not let go!

Fly to PAGE 24.

You follow the cobblestone path toward the blue house. It's bit smaller than the other four homes, you notice. A blue jay perches on the doorknob, then flutters away as you reach for the bell.

Well, you think. This looks nice. The door swings open. You hold out your bag. "Trick or tr —"

The words die on your lips. Because standing right before you . . .

Is your very own family!

"Hello there!" your father cries, slapping your back. "Good to see you!"

"Just in time for supper!" your mother coos. "I made your favorite!"

And then you feel something wet on your face. Could it be? Did your little sister just give you . . . a kiss?

"I missed you," she says. "And so did Champion!"

Your sister's obnoxious white poodle — the poodle that you hate with all your heart — jumps into your arms and begins licking your face!

This is the weirdest thing in the history of the world! How did your family get into this blue house? And why are they being so nice?

Go on to PAGE 30 and find out.

"ROOOOOAAARRRRR!"

The Thing opens the door to the chute. He swipes his paw inside!

But you're already far from his grasp! You climb up, up, up . . . until you reach a small door, push through, and tumble into a fancy bathroom.

Got to get to the first floor, you think. Got to find a way out of this crazy house! You dash into the hallway.

A low snarl sounds from the staircase. Oh, no! The Thing must be headed upstairs!

Time for a change in plans. You run for the elevator and press DOWN.

You're headed to the gym!

Hurry on to PAGE 94.

Forget it. You're out of here. This isn't the county fair, after all. This house could really be haunted! You rush toward the door.

But it slams shut!

The sound of soft, mischievous laughter meets your ears. Where is it coming from?

Heart pounding, you grab the doorknob. You shake it. Locked! You pound the door with your fists.

"Help!" you cry. "Help!"

But the only thing that hears you is the swarm of bats hanging from the ceiling.

They shriek at the sound of your voice. Uh-oh. Looks like you woke them up!

They swoop down from the rafters, flapping their wings, baring their needle-sharp fangs. They're headed right for you!

You fall to the ground, screaming.

Too bad. Looks as if this Halloween adventure drove you totally *batty* in

THE END.

You reach for the skewer.

"All right, Billington!" you cry, pointing the weapon at him. "Let me out of here!"

The captain laughs. "You don't scare me," he says.

He takes a step toward you. Then another.

You don't want to hurt anyone, but know that you've got to make your move! You raise the skewer. Your hand is shaking. But you manage to lunge forward. . . .

The skewer rips through Billington's clothing. And . . .

POP! What was that noise?

WHOOOOSH! You can't believe your eyes. Billington is — *deflating!*

"Noooo!" he screeches. "You punctured me! Noooo!"

You watch as Billington gets shorter and shorter. His form shrivels before your eyes. Until he's nothing but a puddle on the floor.

Whoa! That was totally bizarre. You'd like to know exactly what happened here, but you're not about to stick around to find out. You tear out of the front door and spot a path leading to the white mansion.

You decide to head for it. Maybe someone there can show you the way out of this freaky place.

Go to PAGE 108.

You rise to your feet. Cautiously.

"Thanks," you say. "But I think I have enough candy." You make a move to leave.

The bear frowns. He quickly blocks your path. And growls.

"Heh-heh. Nice bear," you say. You turn to walk the other way. Again, the bear lurches around you to block your path.

You stare at the bear's face. Uh-oh. Now he looks angry! Angry that you don't want to follow him!

The bear rises to his back legs and bares his teeth.

"ROOOOOAAAARRRR!"

Ahhhhhhhhhhhhhhhh!

Silly you. You should have known better. Who would really want to offend a huge polar bear?

Now the bear has decided that *he's* in the mood for a Halloween treat. . . .

Too bad that treat is you!

THE END

"Uh — I'll take the tour," you tell the second elf. "How about if you show me the way out of Sunshine Court?"

"Not until you get the tour!" the elf growls in his deep, gravelly voice.

He grabs you with his claws and drags you to a stone doorway. He pulls you down a stone spiral staircase. With each step the air gets colder, the light dimmer. An occasional mouse scurries across your feet in search of food.

Your stomach clenches. What exactly is going on here? What have you gotten yourself into? Is the elf actually some guy in an incredibly real costume? If not — what is he?

"I'm about to show you the most special room in the house!" your guide exclaims. He takes the steps two at a time. "A room made just for you!"

The elf stops by a large wooden door. He fiddles with a set of keys and sticks one in the lock. Your heart starts pounding in your throat. You get the feeling there's something horrible behind that door!

The elf pushes it open. And pushes you into the room!

Go to PAGE 114.

SLAM! The oven door shuts! It's pitch-dark. You pound on the hard walls.

"Let me out!" you cry.

For a moment you hear nothing. Except a click. Suddenly, the oven begins to get warmer.

Billington is baking you alive!

No doubt about it: Your goose is about to be seriously cooked!

Too bad. You really got burned by this ending.

THE END

You grab the map and stuff it in your trick-or-treat bag. Then you tear across the frozen wasteland.

When you're pretty sure you've left the polar bear far behind, you take out the map and study it. You search for the markers on the map that lead to your escape vehicle.

A huge, snow-covered boulder rises up in front of you. Yes! That's where the map says the sled is hidden! You rush forward to the other side of the rock. A huge shape covered with canvas sits on the other side.

The sled! There it is!

You pull the canvas off of it and hop on.

Then you gasp! How could you be so dumb? You forgot about sled dogs! You can't use this kind of sled without them!

You glance back toward the caves. It's too far! You'll never get back before dark. And the temperature is dropping by the second, getting colder and colder.

"Help!" you cry. The wind howls back at you.

As you feel your body freezing up, you realize — you should have known to stay in the cave!

But, look on the bright side. Didn't you always want to be one of the *cool* kids in your class? Well, now you're the coolest!

THE END

The right door looks good.

You throw it open. The room is totally dark. You see the dim outline of something strange on the table.

You squint . . . and gasp at what you see!

A room of heads lying in a row on a table!

Another one of Hillenthrobben's weird experiments!

Gross! You're out of here! You reach for the door. . . .

SLAM! It shuts in your face!

CLICK! It locks!

You pull at the doorknob.

"Noooo!" You howl with fear. "Let me go!"

"Ha ha ha ha!" Someone laughs. But aren't you alone in the room?

You turn toward the table. No! It can't be! The heads — they're alive! And they're laughing!

"Ha ha ha ha!" Your head throbs with the unearthly sound. The laughter — it's killing you!

"Ha ha ha ha!"

You hit your knees and hold your ears. "Noooo!"

Looks like your trick-or-tricking adventure is over. But start again on *PAGE 1* and maybe you'll have a better idea of how to get a-*head* in this game!

THE END

"Wow!" you whisper. The real Santa! What an amazing treat! You tap Santa's velvety red shoulder. "I wanted to say thank you." You stop short when Santa turns around.

His face! It's isn't jolly and rosy anymore! It's — it's monstrous!

Santa has transformed into a creature from beyond the grave!

His face is a bare skull. A handful of wiry hair grows from the head. Then you see a fat worm crawl out of his right eye!

"Ahhhh!" you shout. The sight makes you want to hurl.

"He-he-he-he-he!" the fake Santa cackles. He whips the reindeer, who climb higher into the night.

The air around you becomes colder. Maybe you should try jumping out of the sleigh. You peer over the edge. No way! You're too high. You'll never survive the fall!

"He-he-he! Happy Halloween!" the Santa-creature screeches. With a quick flick of his forearm he pushes you out of the sleigh!

"Aaaaah!" You hurtle toward a certain death.

Too bad. You thought being saved by Santa would be a real *treat*. But instead, you were *tricked* in

THE END.

Forget the pool. Besides, what if the monster can swim? If you jumped in the pool, you'd be a sitting duck!

You crash through the door and fly down a hallway. You find yourself in . . .

A laundry room!

Before you is a giant washer-and-dryer. On the other side of the room is the bottom of the laundry chute.

If you hurry, you can hide before the Thing finds you!

You'll never fit in the washer, you realize. So what's it going to be? The dryer or the chute?

If you hide in the dryer, go to PAGE 34.
If you hide in the chute, go to PAGE 36.

20

You reach into your candy bag and pull out the long piece of red licorice. The mouse leaps through the air. It grabs the candy out of your hands and gobbles it down.

"Licorice!" it cries. "That's what I call a meal!"

Then it lets out a loud burp and disappears through a tiny hole in the wall.

Oh, no! Is the mouse leaving you here? Your knees go weak at the thought. But seconds later, the door to the room swings open and the mouse jumps out of the keyhole.

"I could make a fortune as a safecracker," it says. "I'd spend all my dough on licorice." Then it points over its shoulder, down the hallway, to a stone door. "There's your way out."

You run down the hall and throw your shoulder against the door. Soon you're standing outside on a green lawn. For a moment you aren't sure where you are. But then you turn and see a giant white mansion, sitting on a small hill.

Turn to PAGE 108.

The Thing roars again. Nathan reaches through the bars and pats him on the head.

"The Thing likes to play games," Nathan continues. "Hide-and-seek is his favorite. And you know what? He wants to play right now. With you!"

"He does?" The Thing snarls at you. Gulp! He doesn't look like a very good sport.

"I'll give you a one-minute head start," Nathan states. "If you can stay alive for an hour, you win. I'll give you all the candy you can eat and let you go. But if the Thing catches you, it's all *he* can eat."

"You — you're crazy!" you stutter.

Nathan starts to giggle again.

"Why are you doing this?" you demand.

"All I wanted was to be your friend!" Nathan yells. "But you won't hang out with me. You think I'm a nerd!"

Whoa! Talk about an overreaction!

Nathan reaches for the latch on the Thing's cage.

"We can hang out from now on!" you tell Nathan. "I promise! Every day!"

"Too little, too late," Nathan replies. He closes his eyes and begins to count. "One, two, three, four . . ."

Aaaaah! Stop standing there and get going to PAGE 123!

Why not walk the dog? It's better than home-work!

Champion pulls you out the door to the center of Sunshine Court. What a weird Halloween, you think. You're stuck walking a stupid, mangy . . .

"GRRRRRRRR! GRRRRRRRRRR!"

Whoa! Champion's wimpy bark is suddenly a deep, ferocious growl. What's that about?

"Hey there, buddy. What are you growling at?" you ask. "It's just me. Your friend . . ."

The tiny little poodle balances on his back legs and bares a set of giant, razor-sharp teeth!

He leaps at you. Straight for your neck.

Turn to PAGE 125.

Your sister is the piano player in your family, and you could never get the hang of the guitar.

That leaves the tuba. But you've never played a tuba in your life!

"ROOOOOAAAAARRRRR!"

The power of the Thing's growl practically blows you back against the wall.

It's the tuba or death! You try to lift it. Man! It's even heavier than you thought!

The Thing licks his lips. Then he takes another step toward you!

You tilt the tuba to your mouth. This better work!

BLAAAAEEERRRTTTTTTTTTT!

You blow into the tuba. And produce one of the ugliest sounds ever! The Thing holds his ears and howls in agony.

BBBBKKKLLLLRRREEEEAAAYYYTTT!

You blow again. This sound is even worse. The Thing drops to his knees and rolls on the floor.

Hey! Now's your chance. Run for it!

The game room! you decide. I'll duck in there!

Get going to PAGE 5.

Lucky for you, the bird keeps its grip. It pumps its wings with all its might. Soon the jungle disappears. You fly over an ocean. Then over a small town. And then . . .

Over Bergen Street to *your* house. Yes! You're safe and sound outside of Sunshine Court!

The bird swoops to your front walk and sets you down!

You have no idea how the bird knew where to take you — but you're not about to ask any questions. "Thanks!" you gush.

The bird squawks as if to say, "You're welcome." Then it lifts off and quickly disappears from view.

Whoa! That was one creepy Halloween adventure, you think. You glance at your watch. Hmmm. Eight-thirty.

You could still go out trick-or-treating, but — nah! You've had enough of this birdbrained holiday, anyway.

THE END

You pick the ghost and — wow! You are dancing!

Actually, you think, this is fun!

The ghost is a great partner. Talk about light on your feet! You flip the ghost into the air. The crowd claps.

But as the ghost comes down the room goes quiet. Dead quiet. What's going on? You glance around and see a huge man in a pirate costume looming over you. He has three black teeth and a bandanna around his neck.

"What're you doing with my ghostie, me hearty?" he demands. His breath smells like year-old garbage.

"Just dancing," you manage to squeak.

"Dancing, aye?" He draws his sword and presses the blade to your neck. It slices a small hole in your collar. Hey! Isn't this guy taking his pirate thing a bit too far?

"No one dances with me ghostie — unless you can pay the price for your dance!" he bellows.

The price? What price? You'd pay anything to get away from this lunatic!

"He loves apples," the ghost tells you. "Give him one! Quickly!"

Did you take the apple from Santa? Go to PAGE 133.

If you didn't, go to PAGE 35.

It sure is weird, putting your life in the hands of a giant polar bear. But then, what else can you do? You cautiously grab the candy and stuff it in your bag. The bear smiles again. Then he waves a paw at you. It looks as if the bear wants you to follow him. Everything that's happened to you today is weird. Why not go with the flow?

The two of you trudge through the frozen wasteland together.

Brrrrr! A vampire costume doesn't do much against arctic temperatures! You know you won't be able to withstand this weather for much longer.

Soon the bear stops by two small caves in the face of an icy rock shelf. The cave on the right is shaped like a heart. The one on the left looks like a four-leaf clover.

The bear points to the caves, as if to say, "Pick one." Then he lopes away, leaving you alone in the middle of a frozen wasteland!

He doesn't have to tell you twice. You're frozen down to your toenails. All you want to do is get some shelter in one of the caves and hope that the bear returns.

But which cave?

If you choose the heart-shaped cave, go to PAGE 116.

If you choose the four-leaf clover, go to PAGE 42.

Toys! It's filled with toys!

"You like it?" the elf asks. He picks up a football and tosses it into the air. "Santa knows what a good kid you've been this year. That's right! He keeps track! So you've won the grand prize! All these toys are for you!"

Whoa! If there's one thing you like better than Halloween candy, it's Christmas toys! You give a broad grin as the elf passes you the football.

"Excellent catch!" he shouts. "Well, enjoy your goodies! They'll make your tomb so much more fun."

Huh? Turn to PAGE 135.

You throw open the door to the left. You look up and gasp. Standing before you is Samson! Hillen-throbben's pet gorilla!

You turn to run. But the door has locked behind you! You're stuck!

"Please," you say. "Don't hurt me."

To your surprise, Samson raises his eyebrow. "Hurt you?" he says. "I want to help you escape."

You gasp. Is this gorilla actually speaking to you?

"H-h-help me?" you stammer.

"That's right," the ape says. He holds out his enormous hand. "Shake?"

You raise your trembling hand and touch his. He gives you a firm, but nice, handshake.

"You'll really help me get away?" you ask.

Samson smiles. His teeth are surprisingly white. "Of course. But I was wondering if, in return, I might have some of your candy?"

Find out if today's your lucky day. Did you leave your bag of candy at the lab or remember to take it with you? Flip a coin!

Heads: You remembered the candy. Go to PAGE 88.

Tails: Oops! You forgot it! Go to PAGE 126.

Nathan leads you through a marble foyer, past a living room as big as a basketball court, to . . .

An elevator? Whoa! You never knew Nathan's family was this loaded!

"It's a fun little house," Nathan tells you as you ride up. "We've got everything! A swimming pool! A gym! A music room! Even a game room with bumper cars!"

The elevator dings. "Ah, here we are. Fourth floor," Nathan says proudly.

He scurries down a wide hallway, then stops and giggles in that nerdy way of his. He pushes the door open to a dark room.

"Come in!" he cries.

You hesitate a moment but then follow him in.

"Okay," you say in the darkness. "Where's the candy?"

SLAM! The door shuts.

CLICK! It locks.

And then . . . you hear a terrifying *ROAR!*

Uh-oh. Go to PAGE 118.

Weird! The inside of the blue house looks exactly like your house at home! Down to the color of the curtains! Down to the green stain you made on the living room sofa when your science project exploded on it.

"Your father and I decided we liked this neighborhood better, so we moved," your mom says. "Surprised?"

Surprised? That's an understatement. But weren't you just thinking that this is the kind of place your parents would love to live in?

"Hey!" your dad calls. "Who's hungry?"

Moments later you're chowing down your favorite meal: a hamburger, fries, and a chocolate milk shake. Cool! Your mom hardly ever makes this stuff for you!

"Delicious!" you say, noisily sucking up the last of your shake with a straw. "Thanks, Mom and Dad. Well, guess I'd better get back to my trick-or-treating."

"Trick-or-treating?" your mother says. Her smile is so wide it has a sort of weird look about it. "I think you've had enough of that. You have two choices. Either play games with us here in the living room — or it's bedtime!"

Like your mom said, make your choice.
If you hit the sack, go to PAGE 74.
If you play games, go to PAGE 60.

You can't move your legs! You feel as if you're standing in a giant tub of glue.

Terrified, you scream at the top of your lungs. "Help!"

"Caw! Caw! . . . Cheep! Cheep!" Comes the answer to your cry.

Only monkeys and birds are around to hear you!

You sink to your waist! Then your chest! Your arms are stuck at your sides! The wet sand is an inch from your mouth. . . .

You gasp. . . .

And swallow a mouthful of quicksand!

Sorry. Looks like your chance of surviving is totally *sunk*.

THE END

You dive under the pool table.

Seconds later the Thing lets you know he's here by tossing a Ping-Pong table halfway across the room. Your stomach clenches with fear.

CRASH!

The Thing mows over a video game.

BOOM!

He chops another Ping-Pong table in half with his fist!

You squeeze your eyes shut, and pray the monster doesn't see or hear you. Yes! The Thing heads away from you toward the bumper cars. A lucky break! In another second you'll be able to make a run for it.

Just as you are poised to tear for the door, the Thing wheels around. He sniffs the air and growls.

Then the monster begins to stalk . . .

Straight toward you!

Try to defend yourself on PAGE 77.

You're no wimp! Would you read all those *Goosebumps* books if you were? You know the smart thing would be to run — but you've got to check out those footsteps!

You draw in a breath and take a step forward.

The floor groans. You take another careful step. Wait a minute! Why do you suddenly feel you're being watched?

Heart pounding, you wheel around.

No one's there. Only the grinning skeleton.

Get a grip, you tell yourself. This place is so obviously scary-looking that it has to be a fake.

You take a breath and march across the room. There, sitting on a wooden desk, wrapped in a red ribbon, you see a candy bar.

Mmmmm. It looks really good! You find yourself being drawn to it. You *have* to eat it. You stuff half the bar into your mouth in one second flat.

You take a breath. Man, that was *good*. You look at the rest of it. Should you finish the other half now? Or save it for later?

If you save the candy bar, write down on your piece of paper that you still have half a candy bar. If not, eat up! Either way, head to PAGE 78.

The dryer! you decide.

You open its door. Then you curl your body into a tight ball and force yourself in. You slam the door behind you.

From your round little hiding place you hear the crazed monster snarl. He's tracked you here!

"ROOOOOOAAARRRR!"

You gulp. The Thing sounds like he's right in front of the dryer!

Then you feel the Thing pick up the dryer and shake it! A moment later, the monster tears open the dryer door and peers at you with oozy yellow eyes.

He flashes a wicked grin — and slams the door shut!

Weird! you think. What's going on? It doesn't take long for you to find out.

"Ow! Ow! Ow!" you yell. You're being tumbled around. Your arms and legs smash against the metal sides of the dryer. And you're feeling very warm.

Could it be . . . ?

Oh, no!

The Thing has turned on the machine!

Tumble dry on PAGE 95.

You gulp. You don't have an apple. "I — I —" you stutter.

"If you can't pay the price," the pirate cries, "you'll have to pay with your life!"

He pushes you to the floor. The sword flashes through the air. You prepare to feel the blade slice you in two!

But the ghost speaks up: "Stop!"

You gulp. The sword is an inch from your stomach.

"What is it?" the pirate growls.

"Give the vampire a fair fight!" the ghost says.

"Fair fight?" the pirate cries.

The ghost pulls you up. Someone dressed as one of the Three Musketeers hands you a sword.

The pirate frowns. "All right, me hearty. You got your sword. Now stand up so I can rip out your guts!"

What? You don't know how to sword fight!

"Listen," you say. "I'm no good with . . ."

"Prepare to be skewered!" the pirate bellows.

On shaky legs, you rise to your feet. You want to be brave and fight. But maybe it would be smarter to run for your life!

If you stay and fight, go to PAGE 56.
If you run, go to PAGE 51.

You open the door to the laundry chute and dive into a pile of dirty clothes.

"Yuck," you complain. You throw a pair of underwear off your nose.

But you have more to worry about than dirty underwear.

"*RRROOOAAAAR!*" The Thing thrashes into the room and starts to rip it apart. Terrified, you clutch a pile of clothes for comfort. You feel your stomach clench as the Thing stomps your way!

What now?

You glance up. The chute rises up above you. And there's a ladder built into its side.

If you can climb up in time, you might escape!

Get climbing on PAGE 10.

You gaze at the board.

```
B    L    O    O    D
                    E
                    A
                    T
                    H
```

Then you check your letters: *E*, *R*, *A*, *Q*, and *T*. Hmmm . . . This is a toughie!

"I'll give you a hint," your mom says. "Use the *T* that's already on the board to help you spell a five-letter word that has to do with Halloween."

You nod at your mom, then look back at your letters. Can you figure it out?

If you can't come up with the word, go to PAGE 72.

If you can, go to PAGE 89.

You've got to think of a way out of this! Outside the pool, the Thing licks his lips and waits for you to be a sitting duck.

And it won't take long! The shallow end is quickly becoming nothing but a puddle!

The Thing splashes into the water and moves toward you. His hideous mouth opens wide.

There's nothing you can do. No place to hide!

Until you have an idea — a desperate idea.

Maybe the Thing would rather eat some candy than eat you!

You swim to the edge of the pool, root through your bag, and throw candy bars at the monster.

Rats! The Thing bats them away! Dessert isn't on his menu!

Frantic, you reach into the bottom of your bag. . . .

Do you find something there besides candy?

If so, what is it?

If you find a yellow rose, go to PAGE 90.
If you find a length of rope, go to PAGE 92.

Yep. He's definitely lost it.

Captain Billington has transformed from the nicest adult you've ever met into a maniac.

"Move it!" he shouts. He pushes you down a narrow hallway, farther into the green house.

He shoves you into a small study. There is a door on either side of the room. One is round, the other a perfect square. "Go inside!" Billington roars. "Quickly!"

You have no idea which door he wants you to go into, but you're not about to ask. Pick a door and use it.

Hurry!

If you choose the circular door, go to PAGE 82.
If you pick the square door, go to PAGE 91.

Yellow was never your favorite color. But this house has a sweet look about it. It even has a garden of yellow roses out front!

Wow! You can't help noticing how pretty they are.

Maybe you should pick one before you knock on the door? You could give the flower to your mom later. She *loves* yellow roses.

Then again, your mother wouldn't approve of you taking a rose from somebody else's garden, would she?

If you pick the yellow flower, write it down on your piece of paper. But whether you pick the rose or not, go to PAGE 119.

Second floor!

You dash off the elevator and burst through a set of swinging doors. Before you is an Olympic-size swimming pool. The water looks beautiful. Too bad this isn't a good time for a leisurely swim!

"RRRROOOAAAAR!"

Yikes! You hear the Thing coming for you. Okay, you tell yourself. Calm! Stay calm!

But how can you stay calm when a man-eating monster is hot on your heels?

CRASH! The sound comes from the hallway.

The Thing is seconds away!

You glance back at the pool. What if the Thing can't swim? You'll be safe in the water!

Then you spot a door on the other side of the room. If you run like mad, you can just make it!

If you dive in, go to PAGE 104.
If you rush through the door, go to PAGE 19.

A four-leaf clover! The good luck sign. You crawl into the cave away from the wind. And, boy, do you feel lucky to be out of that harsh cold!

Wait a minute, what's going on? You're slipping backwards. You try to reach for a hold, but the entire cave is covered in ice!

"Ahhhhhhhhhhh!" you cry. You slip away from the mouth of the cave and find yourself sliding down a steep hill.

"Ahhhhh!" you scream again, as the floor drops out from under you. You're falling through the air!

Ten feet! Twenty feet! Thirty! *SPLASH!*

You plunge deep into a pool of water. Panicked, you look around, expecting to see nothing but miles of ice.

Then you realize — the water isn't even cold. In fact — aahhh — it's nice and warm!

Whoa! You're in a pond back in Sunshine Court! You don't know how you got there — and you don't care. You're safe — for now. You pull yourself out of the water and sigh with relief.

Before you is the white mansion! You head for it. Maybe someone in there can get you out of this freaky neighborhood!

Go to PAGE 108.

You cram a peanut bar in your mouth. Then a Tootsie Roll. Then a giant piece of chocolate. Then your favorite! A Double-Chocolate-Triple-Caramel Delight! You eat for a half an hour, take a break, then eat some more.

That's when you start to feel funny. Your knees wobble so much you sit on the floor. You clutch your stomach.

The door to the room swings open. Dr. Hillenthrobben waddles in and slaps you on the back.

"What's the matter?" he cries. "Don't tell me you're sick? I want you to eat my candy all night long!"

Eat candy all night? Right now, you'd rather die!

"Please," you whisper. "Take me home!"

Dr. Hillenthrobben shakes his head. "Sorry," he says. "Samson! Continue the experiment!"

He snaps his fingers. The gorilla appears at the doorway and scoops a bunch of candy in his hands. What's this? He forces your mouth wide open! No! Not more!

"Bottoms up!" Hillenthrobben shrieks madly.

Oh, no! You are forced to chew and chew all night long . . . till you've eaten yourself to death.

Well, Mom always told you too much candy was no good for you. But you never knew how right she was!

THE END

You tear across the room and jump into a blue bumper car. There's just one minor problem: The Thing sees you!

There's only one thing to do — drive this bumper car to freedom!

You start the car and rev up the engine. Wow! Inside, it looks like a *real* car!

The Thing gallops toward you.

You stomp on the accelerator....

But the car doesn't move!

Nooooooo!

Go to PAGE 84.

The door shuts behind you as you follow the man down the winding hall. Wow! He's really in a hurry. You have to take two steps for every one of his.

"Ah, but I'm being rude!" he cries, as he veers left down the hall. "I'm R. J. Josiah Billington! You can call me Captain Billington, if you like. I always wanted to be a captain. Trouble is, I hate the sea!"

Okay. That settles it. This guy is weird! Maybe you don't want to be in his house after all, you decide. But you're too curious to turn around. You want to see what's making that yummy-smelling purple smoke.

Captain Billington pulls to an abrupt halt by a large brass door.

"You're going to love this room!" he practically shouts to you. "All the children do! This is going to be your best Halloween ever!"

Head into the room on PAGE 130.

"Hey! Let me out of here!"

You pull on the heavy wooden door. It won't budge. Maybe the elf guy is still out there. Maybe he's just playing a joke, you think.

"Hello?" you shout. "This isn't funny! Let me out!"

You press your ear to the wooden door. No response.

You're trapped!

Sweat breaks out on your forehead. Maybe you heard that elf right in the first place. Maybe this is your tomb!

"Yo! Buddy!"

You glance around. Where did that voice come from?

"Over here!"

"Who are you?" you demand. "Where are you?"

"What are you, blind? I'm down here!"

You glance down, and — on top of a basketball — you see a mouse standing on its hind legs.

You stare at it. Could the voice have come from it?

"That's right, Einstein," the mouse says. "I'm talking to you. Now, if you want to get out of here, give me a piece of red licorice and I'll help you!"

Check your trick-or-treat bag. If you have a piece of red licorice, go to PAGE 20.

If you don't, turn to PAGE 75.

Trembling, you lean forward and see . . .

Nathan!

Reading a large book!

"Hi," he says, looking up.

"What're you doing here?" you ask suspiciously.

"What do you think?" he replies. "I'm reading."

He holds up a picture of a country landscape showing a knight in shining armor and . . .

POW! From out of nowhere there's a blinding flash!

You shield your eyes. Where did that come from? you wonder. And where did Nathan go? You glance right and left. It's like he disappeared. And needless to say, you don't trust Nathan one bit. You need to find out where he went.

Then you hear a voice. "Hey! Down here!"

"Where are you?" you cry, trembling.

"Down here!"

What? You glance at the floor. The book he had lies there — open to the page he was reading. You glance at the picture on the page, and see Nathan standing next to the knight, waving at you! Whoa! What's up with that?

Find out on PAGE 106.

Thief or not, you're taking Dr. Gildenblithen's advice and getting out of there!

You squeeze your way through the open window, and you are gone!

"Good-bye," you call to Gildenblithen. "Uhh — good luck with the stealing!"

"Thanks," the doctor calls back. He gives you a thumbs-up sign.

You turn, and see the red cobblestone path in front of you. You follow it through a thicket of trees, and see the white mansion rise up before you!

Excellent! Maybe someone in there can help you get out of Sunshine Court!

Go on to PAGE 108.

Go back into the bitter cold? No way, José! You prefer hanging out with a bunch of skeletons to freezing to death!

You cuddle up and try to keep warm. But you're nervous. If that bear doesn't come back, you're dead meat.

An hour passes. Then another! Where's that bear?

Finally you hear sniffing at the foot of the cave.

The polar bear is back! You rush to the cave's mouth.

Whoa, baby! Talk about *weird*! The polar bear sits in the pilot's seat of an airplane! It's amazing! But at this point you'll believe almost anything!

The bear waves you toward the plane.

You hop in, buckle your seat belt, and watch the bear step on the gas. You roar down the arctic ice and — you're airborne!

You have no idea where the bear learned how to fly, but some things just shouldn't be explained, you decide.

The bear delivers you back to your home. You wave good-bye and glance at your watch. Wait! It's still early! You've still got time to go out and collect some candy!

Looks like you're going to have a Happy Halloween after all!

THE END

50

You'll take the Thing over whatever Nathan's cooked up in his warped mind any day. You decide to do battle.

The knight gives you a spear. Then he whistles. Another horse gallops up. You hop on and follow the knight across the plain. Your hands are so sweaty with fear you have trouble holding the reins. But you have to have courage. You have to face the Thing.

You ride for miles and miles until you reach a large mountain.

"The Thing lives up there," the knight says.

You guide your horses up the steep mountain path. The path ends at the mouth of a large cave. Then you see a bright light! And the Thing lumbers out of the cave.

Only he's not quite the same.

He's huge! Twice as big as he was before. The Thing opens his jaws — and you realize where the bright light came from. It's a flame! A flame the Thing is shooting out of his mouth!

The Thing rises onto his hind legs. He towers over you! He opens his tremendous mouth.

Oh, no! You're going to be toast!

Burn it out on PAGE 129.

This is no time to be a hero!

You throw down your sword and cut through the crowd. You can hear the pirate's footsteps right behind you. At any second his sword may cut you in two! You turn a corner and spy a door. Quickly, you yank it open and duck into a dark room.

A wave of relief washes over you. Safe! But then you hear a rustling sound. Someone's in the room with you!

You feel along the wall and flip a light switch.

What? Two vampires! Standing over an open coffin? You gasp and take a step back.

Get real, you tell yourself. They're just two guys dressed up for Halloween like you.

Then the first vampire smiles, showing off a pair of six-inch fangs. They look like they're — dripping with blood!

You're frozen, too terrified to say a word. But then you blurt out: "A pirate is trying to kill me!"

The vampires exchange a glance. Then the second one smiles. "We'll be glad to help," he says. "Do you have a mango lollipop?"

Quick! Look inside your trick-or-treat bag!
If you have the lollipop, go to PAGE 83.
If you don't, go to PAGE 79.

52

You dash into the steam room. Thick, white fog billows around you and fills the room with wet heat.

You hurry to the back of the little room and hunt for a place to hide. It's so steamy you can't see. So you stretch out your arms to make sure you won't walk into the wall.

But wait — you can't feel any wall!

Big steam room! you think. You keep on walking.

Soon the steam begins to clear. The hard floor you're walking on turns soft.

What is going on?

Then you make out the dim outlines of trees.

"CAW! CAW!"

A giant, colorful bird swoops over your head! You duck in the nick of time.

Ahead, a monkey leaps from tree to tree.

Whoa!

It looks as if you're in — a jungle!

Huh? Turn to PAGE 55.

You try to reply but your voice catches in your throat.

"Come, child. What is it you want? I'm a busy man!" A figure steps from the shadows. You see a short, squat man, wearing a white lab coat. He has a huge handlebar mustache, and he wears a purple necktie that dangles to his knees. "Dr. Hillenthrobben's the name," he introduces himself.

"Uh, trick-or-treat?" you say shyly.

Dr. Hillenthrobben narrows his eyes at you.

"I know why you're here!" he exclaims. "Dr. Gildenblithen sent you to steal my experiments! I knew it!"

"Wait!" you say. "I've never heard of . . ."

Before you can finish, Dr. Hillenthrobben wheels around. "SAMSON!" he cries.

In an instant an enormous gorilla fills the entire doorway!

A wave of fear rushes over you.

"Bring the child inside, Samson!" Hillenthrobben says.

No choice: You have to go with Hillenthrobben to PAGE 6!

54

Who will answer the door, you wonder?

Horrible thoughts fill your head. You imagine a werewolf with razor-sharp teeth. Or a zombie who will rip your head off! Or a . . .

The door opens!

You blink, utterly floored.

There's no werewolf.

No monster!

Standing before you is the last person you ever expected to see. . . .

Who? Who? *Find out on PAGE 101.*

Somehow, you've ended up in the heart of a jungle!

You'd love to take time to wonder how this happened — but you're too worried about the Thing. He could burst into this scene at any second!

You spot a tall tree to your left. If you climb it you can scout out the best way to go.

But what if the Thing appears by the tree and waits for you to come down? Then you'll be deader than dead.

Maybe it's best to get running!

If you run for it, go to PAGE 71.
If you climb the tree, go to PAGE 109.

You're no coward!

"All right," you shout. "Let's rumble!"

The pirate smiles, exposing a row of crooked brown teeth. "With pleasure!" he says.

The crowd forms a tight circle so there's no-where to run. You point your sword. The pirate laughs.

You lunge toward him, but the pirate steps out of the way. He's faster than you thought!

"You'll have to do better than that!" he yells. "Come at me again!"

You turn to the pirate and point the sword. Here goes nothing!

You lunge forward. . . .

But the pirate flicks his wrist . . .

Too bad.

You've just become a vampire-kabob!

Looks like you really got *stuck* with a bad

END.

A wave of dry heat smacks you in the face as you close the sauna door.

Man, it's hot in here! Your mouth goes bone-dry. You spot a heavy piece of metal pipe on a bench. Maybe you should grab it and stand by the door. That way, if the Thing comes in, you'll be ready.

You also spot a mirror, lying on one of the benches in the sauna. What could that be for? you wonder.

Your heart pounds and pounds out the seconds as you wait. Sweat drips down your forehead. Will the Thing find you here? If he does, what will he do to you?

A second passes.

Then another . . .

Outside, you hear metal screeching. It sounds as if the Thing is tearing apart the lockers looking for you! His roar shakes the inside of the sauna.

Then you hear footsteps coming close to the door. You hear a loud sniffing sound. Then, oh, no! The doorknob! The Thing is tearing it off the door!

The door slams open and the Thing thunders in!

Quick! Grab something to defend yourself!

If you grab the pipe, go to PAGE 64.
If you pick up the mirror, go to PAGE 121.

A light flicks on and you find yourself in a white room. White walls, white floor, and white ceiling. And no furniture.

But what's that? You hear something behind you. You wheel around and realize you're sharing the room with a tall man with a gray goatee and thick black glasses.

"Dr. Gildenblithen's the name," he says.

Dr. Gildenblithen? Dr. Hillenthrobben mentioned him! He thought you were Gildenblithen's spy!

"Dr. Hillenthrobben thinks you're trying to steal his work," you tell the man.

"He's right!" the doctor exclaims, eyes wide. "I'm here to steal something right now!"

Whoa! you think. Then you realize something. "Wait a minute, aren't you a prisoner here too?" you ask.

"I'm only pretending to be a prisoner," Gildenblithen explains. "But you can get out! Just hop through that window!"

Yes! you think. An escape! Then again, this guy's a crook. Should you trust him?

If you hop through the window, go to PAGE 48.
If you stay in the room, go to PAGE 131.

You burst out of the elevator on the first floor. You look right and left. Then you tear down the main hallway. You see a music room on your right. But forget that! Straight ahead is the front door!

You grab the doorknob and pull.

It's locked!

You feel a sharp wave of panic. Stay calm. Stay calm, you order yourself, and look around.

Yes! A window!

You try it. It's nailed shut! Desperate, you look around for something to smash the glass. You know the Thing can't be far behind.

"ROOOOOOAAAARRRRRR!"

You wheel around!

The Thing is at the end of the hall.

He hasn't seen you, but he's coming your way! Quick! Duck into the music room!

Better hurry on to PAGE 132.

Bed? No way. You want to keep an eye on your family. They're acting way too weird for your comfort.

In seconds, your father clears the dining room table, and your mother lays out a game called Word Mix.

Ugh, you think. A word game. You hate word games!

But you've got to play along till you find out what's going on here. You take a seat and pick five letters. Soon your sister lays down the first word.

B-L-O-O-D.

"Blood?" you say. "That's a bizarre first word."

"What's wrong with *blood*?" your mom asks. You don't like the way she lingers over the word. As if she loves saying it. "And here's my first word!" she says.

Your mom arranges her letters on the board. Using the *D* from your sister's BLOOD she spells: DEATH.

"Death?" you cry. Now you're really freaked out.

"What's the matter with *death*?" your dad asks with a wink. "Hey! Everybody does it!"

As your family laughs, a chill shoots from your pinky toes to the top of your head. This is *weird*!

"Come on!" your sister says to you. "Your turn!"

Take your turn on PAGE 37.

This guy's not touching your teeth! You break for the door.

But Billington is too fast. In a single motion he grabs you and throws you on the chair!

He straps you in!

"Noooooooooooooo!" you cry, shaking with terror.

The captain laughs. He glances at your mouth.

"I see two cavities already!"

Then he reaches behind him.

WHHHHHHHIIIIRRRRRRRRRRRRRRRR!

Yikes! Is that a drill?

Oh, well. Your mom always warned you that eating too much candy would ruin your teeth.

Open wide . . .

and say . . .

THE END!

The heavy cue ball flies toward the Thing's mouth. . . .

Closer and closer . . . until . . .

It is an inch from smashing in his teeth! Got him, you think! He won't be able to eat me without any choppers!

But the Thing raises his paw.

And catches the ball!

Oh, no! You want to run but you're frozen with fear. The Thing cranes his neck and howls. You shiver to your bones.

Please make it fast, you think. One quick bite and good-bye!

You shut your eyes tightly.

A moment passes. . . .

And then another . . .

Slowly, you open your eyes again.

What's this? The Thing is examining the ball. Then he meets your eyes and appears to smile.

The Thing waves at you.

It looks like he wants you to go out for a pass!

Better do it on PAGE 65.

Up close, the orange house looks more like a shack. You sure don't expect such a run-down dump to have a lot in the way of candy. But you figure it's worth a try.

KNOCK! KNOCK! KNOCK!

"Trick-or-treat," you call.

You wait. And wait. Nothing.

KNOCK! KNOCK! KNOCK!

"TRICK-OR-TREAT!" you shriek.

Again, you wait. A light breeze rustles through a wind chime, and eerie bells fill the early evening air.

That's it. You're out of here. You turn to go.

CREEEAAAAAKKKK...

You glance over your shoulder. The rickety wood door swings open. By itself!

You swallow hard. What's there? A ghost or something?

"Greetings!" a creepy voice cries from inside the darkened house. "What is it you want?"

Find out who's speaking on PAGE 53.

You grab the heavy pipe. The Thing rears up on his hind legs. You swing the pipe backwards, ready to clobber him.

He lunges for you!

And trips!

WHAM! He hits the floor with a thundering noise. He lies there. Still. Silent.

Yes! The Thing is out cold!

You spy the sauna's temperature control on the wall. It gives you a great idea! You spin it all the way to high. As the Thing begins to stir, you rush out and bolt the door. This time with the heavy metal bolt on the outside.

Whew! You lean against the sauna door and suck in the cool air.

BOOM! You're thrown off the door as the Thing slams into it.

Will the door hold? Find out on PAGE 85.

You begin running. Then you turn and wave for the ball. You half expect the Thing's mighty throw to knock you over. To your surprise the monster tosses the ball gently — and right to you!

"Good one," you say.

Now it's his turn. The mighty monster lumbers past a row of Ping-Pong tables, then cuts directly across the enormous room. You take aim and throw. . . .

The Thing leaps into the air and snags the ball with his right paw.

"Yes!" you shout. Wow! The Thing is a great athlete!

"What's going on here?" a voice demands.

You turn. It's Nathan.

"I command you to destroy this kid!" Nathan yells at the Thing.

The Thing swipes a sharp-clawed paw at Nathan. He lets out a threatening roar.

"My creation," Nathan whines. "He was supposed to kill you, but now you've ruined him! He *likes* you!"

"Too bad," you reply. You send another long pass the Thing's way. "Instead of killing, it looks like the Thing would rather *catch* some Halloween spirit!"

THE END

You creep to the door. An image of your father turning into a giant insect flashes into your mind. You grasp the doorknob with a shaking hand and pull open the door. . . .

But what's that you hear? *Singing?*

You tiptoe down the hall and peer into the living room. No! Your mother is playing the piano. And your sister and father are singing along at the top of their lungs! Owwww! The sound is so awful, it's hurting your ears.

"Join us!" your father cries, turning your way.

Your mother bangs the piano even louder. Your sister belts for all she's worth. Even Champion howls. Then the terrifying finale: Your father begins to harmonize!

You hit your knees, clutching your ears.

"No!" you cry. "Stop! Stop!"

"Sorry," Mom calls over the noise. "We're so happy about the new place, we just have to sing!"

"The hills are alive with the sound of music!" your dad croaks.

And so is your house. Alive with ear-wrenching show tunes! *For all eternity!*

Seems like you were right, this whole set up *was* too good to be true!

THE END

You can't say that you really trust Nathan. But fighting the Thing? Why would you volunteer for that?

So you follow Nathan down a dirt road and soon blend into a crowd. Everyone is dressed like they are part of King Arthur's Court.

"You're going to love this!" Nathan coos. "I've got a special surprise lined up."

Hmmm . . . The surprises you've gotten so far this night haven't been much fun. You think about running. But where to? You don't even know where you are!

Then you feel someone grab your cape.

"That's him!" a deep voice says. "Get him!"

Nathan laughs. "See you later!"

"Wait!" you cry. But it's too late. Two knights push you down a stone hallway. You don't know where they're taking you, but you sure know it isn't good!

They open a door and push you through.

You hear a crowd cheer! You look around — and gasp. You're *in* the arena! And at the other end of the field, you see the Thing on a horse! And he's holding a giant lance!

Get out of this one on PAGE 80.

You hate science class! No way do you want to sacrifice your life for that stuff! But you can't escape.

Samson carries you back to the lab in his mighty arms. He straps you onto the operating table — again!

Dr. Hillenthrobben pulls open a curtain. Behind it, you see an alligator, about eight feet long!

"Ahhh!" you cry. What's Hillenthrobben going to do, feed you to that thing?

The doctors place wires on your body. Then they do the same to the alligator. Wait a minute, what's going on here?

The doctors nod to each other. Then Gildenblithen reaches up over his head and pulls an orange lever.

Noooo! Electricity pounds through your body. But that's not the worst part.

Your arms begin to shrink into little reptile claws. You feel your teeth push out of your gums and become large and sharp. Green scales cover your entire body!

Are you being turned into the first living human-reptile? You got it. And you've also reached the end of this book.

See you later, alligator!

THE END

You step into the house and find yourself inside a giant ballroom filled with monsters, witches, and vampires.

Great costumes, you think. They look totally real.

A shiver runs through you. It's silly, you know, but part of you thinks that maybe they look a little *too* real.

Hey, you have your candy. Maybe you should just get out of here. You turn — and find your path blocked by two elves. Not real elves, you reason. Kids in costumes.

Then you notice the elves' hands. They have knife-edged claws at the ends of their fingers! Whoa. These aren't like any elf costumes you've ever seen!

"Where are you going?" the first elf demands. His voice is low and gravelly. Not like a kid's at all. He grabs your cape with one of his claws.

RIIIP! Whoa! The claws are tearing holes in your cape! You gasp. Does that mean they're *real*?

"The party's just starting," the second elf growls.

"Have a drink!" the first elf offers. He holds out a frothing glass of punch.

"No!" the second elf cries, grabbing you. "Follow me! This house is huge! There's so much to see!"

If you follow the second elf, go to PAGE 14.
If you take the punch, go to PAGE 93.

You take a step back, terrified.

"Don't fight it," Billington says soothingly. "Think of the bright side. You'll be part of the most delicious dessert ever made in the history of mankind!"

Baked into a pie? That's not your idea of a bright side. Your mouth is dry. Your legs are weak.

But, wait! There's a long metal skewer on the counter.

Do you pick it up and fight . . . ?

Or make a run for the door?

If you use the skewer, go to PAGE 12.
If you dash for the door, go to PAGE 115.

Forget the tree. The Thing could totally trap you up there! You run for it.

You leap over vines that grow across the muddy forest floor. You try to block out the chatter of wild animals. Who knows what's lurking in this jungle?

But you'd rather take on a whole gang of lions than that horrible Thing! The thought of him sends a chill of terror up your spine.

Soon you reach a small clearing. Okay, you tell yourself. Got to find a place to hide!

You glance around. On the other side of the clearing is a shelf of rocks. You can duck behind there!

You make a move for the rocks.

Or, at least, you try to.

You look down at your feet and gasp in terror.

You're ankle-deep in quicksand!

No, make that knee-deep!

And sinking fast!

Sink on to PAGE 31.

Rats! You can't think of anything!

"The word is TREAT," your sister says. "See?"

```
B    L    O    O    D
                    E
                    A
                    T    R    E    A    T
                    H
```

"Oh, yeah," you say. "Guess I missed it. Speaking of treats, can I go catch up with my buddies now?"

You expect your parents to say "Of course." Instead your father leans forward and frowns.

"No!" he barks. "You missed your word. Now you've got to pay the consequences!"

"Yes!" your mother agrees. "You must suffer!"

You stare at your mom. Suffer? What in the world does she mean? And — wait a minute — your mom would never say something like that! What's going on here?

"Either do extra English homework or take Champion out for a walk!" your father commands.

You sigh and wipe your brow. Homework or dog-walking? Whew. That's not so bad.

If you walk Champion, go to PAGE 22.
If you do your homework, go to PAGE 99.

"ARRRRRAGGGHHHHH!" the Thing cries. He points to the guitar. He wants you to keep playing. Uh-oh.

"The strings broke," you try to explain.

But the monster isn't interested in excuses. He wants music. He growls and paws at the floor. Then he bares his massive teeth.

His claws reach out for you!

You smash the Thing over the head with the guitar. Then you tear by him into the hallway. But he's hot on your heels, furious, thirsting for blood. *Your blood!*

You see a stairwell, and take the steps up two at a time. At the top, you see a door marked: POOL.

You run through the door and find yourself standing by an Olympic-size swimming pool.

Hey! What if the Thing can't swim? Maybe you should dive in!

Then you notice something else — a door at the opposite end of the pool. Maybe you should just keep on running!

If you dive in, go to PAGE 104.
If you rush through the door, go to PAGE 19.

74

Yawn! You're feeling a little sleepy from that heavy meal, so you choose bed.

Ahhh! You lie on warm sheets in your favorite pair of PJs. You dad comes to tuck you in.

"Night, sport," he says. He kisses your cheek.

The light turns out and the room is still. This sure isn't the sort of Halloween you had in mind. In bed so early? But somehow it's worth it. This new house and the new way your family is treating you are both so cool.

You begin to drift off. Until you hear a sound — your father whistling.

That's weird. Your dad never whistles.

A thought flashes in your head. It sends shivers down your spine. *Maybe he's not your real father!*

Turn to PAGE 98.

"I didn't bring any licorice!" you say. You look in your candy bag. "How about some chocolate? Or some caramel? Oh, wait! I think I saw taffy in there."

The mouse shakes its head. "Sorry, buddy. If you want my help, it's got to be red licorice."

"But I can't get you any! I'm locked in!"

The mouse scratches its chin. "Good point. Oh, well, too bad."

The rodent disappears into a hole in the wall. "Wait!" you cry. But it doesn't help. The mouse is gone.

Panicked, you pace the room. If you don't get out of here, you're going to die! You're sure of it.

But, wait! Something catches your eye. A large rock in the wall is sticking out in a strange way. You rush over and push on it. It's loose! Maybe it's a way out!

You pull at that rock with all your might. It crashes to the floor with a loud *THUD*. You peer through the hole in the wall and see a narrow tunnel.

If you suck in your stomach, you can just squeeze through!

Hurry through the tunnel to PAGE 122.

You jump in the elevator and press ONE.

Got to get to the first floor and find a way out, you think. That's your only chance!

But, wait. Why aren't the doors closing?

"Come on!" you shout. You grab the doors and try to press them shut. "Close!"

"*ROOOOOOAAAAR!*"

Oh, no! It's the Thing! He's at the end of the hall. And he's coming for you!

You try to force the doors closed again. Yes! They're closing!

The Thing dives toward you. . . .

Noooo!

He makes it inside just as the doors shut!

You're locked in with the Thing!

There's no escape now. You're going to be a snack for the Thing.

Looks like you've reached a really dead . . .

END.

A line of saliva gushes out of the Thing's mouth to the floor. Your heart pounds faster than a machine gun. This is it! You're a goner! There's no way you can possibly defend yourself.

Unless . . .

You reach up and grab the cue ball.

The Thing bares his teeth and roars. You roll out from under the table and force yourself to your feet. You cock your arm. Hopefully, all those hours of pitching for Little League will come in handy!

The Thing is just feet from you now.

And getting closer!

Come on, you think. Just a little farther!

The monster lets loose a terrifying howl.

But you hold your ground.

The Thing opens his mouth . . . ready to chomp you.

That's when you take aim and throw.

See what happens on PAGE 62.

Now that you've dealt with the candy bar, you decide to explore the rest of the house. Maybe there will be some more candy around, you think.

At the far end of the room, you spot a doorway. You creep over to it. A chill breeze rushes toward you through a crack under the door. What could be in there?

You open the door and step inside.

Whoa! You're blinded by a flash of brilliant white light. You begin shivering all over.

When your eyes adjust to the light, you glance around.

You don't believe it! Snow! You're suddenly knee-deep in it!

Turn to PAGE 111.

"I'm s-sorry," you stammer. "I don't have a lollipop."

WHAM! The pirate breaks down the door. You're dead meat! You close your eyes and wait to feel the pirate's sword.

"Arrrrgghh!" You hear the pirate gurgle. You open your eyes. Whoa! The vampires have bitten the pirate in the neck! They're *real* vampires!

The pirate is out for the count! But before you get to cheer, the vampires lick their lips and take a step toward you. Oh, no! Looks like you're next!

"Are you *sure* you don't have a mango lollipop?" one asks. Blood drips from his teeth.

"Well," you stammer. "I'm, uh . . ."

Before you can finish the other lifts his cape. "I am Count Dracula, and I have come to . . ."

This is it! you think. I'm a vampire snack!

"EAT YOUR CANDY!" the vampire finishes.

You're stunned. "What?" you say. "My . . . *candy*?"

The vampires snatch your bag of goodies and begin to stuff themselves! All you can do is watch in horror as . . .

The vampires eat every last piece of your candy!

AAAARRRRGHHHHHHHH!

THE END

The Thing lets out a giant roar.

His horse snorts twice, then gallops toward you. The point of the Thing's lance is aimed straight for your chest!

Only one thing to do — run to the stands and jump in!

But the crowd lifts you and tosses you back to the vicious Thing.

"Kill!" they cry. "Kill!"

You fall to your knees. "No!" you beg. "Noooo!"

The Thing charges toward you.

He raises his lance!

You close your eyes and await your doom!

The last thing you hear is Nathan's delighted giggle cutting through the noise of the crowd.

"You were always way too mean to me!" Nathan calls. "I tried to tell you that. But maybe now you'll get my *point*!"

THE END

The bear rises to his hind legs and towers over you.

"*ROARRRRRR!*"

"Aaaaah!" You run for your life!

And slip on an icy patch.

FROMP! You land facedown in the snow. Quickly, you roll over. The bear stands over you. He roars again, revealing a massive set of jaws.

You shut your eyes! This is it! You're through!

Then you hear something strange.

SNNNIFF! SNNNIFF! The bear is sniffing at your face.

You peek at the creature out of one eye.

The bear grins, exposing that giant row of teeth. But — weird. He looks as if he's smiling.

He digs at the snow before him, and unearths — a humongous caramel pop. He nudges it toward you with his nose. It sits just a foot away from the bear's heavy, clawed paw. It seems he wants you to take the candy.

Hmmm. Should you trust the ferocious-looking bear?

If you refuse the candy, go to PAGE 13.
If you take it, go to PAGE 26. (And don't forget to write down what you put in your candy bag!)

You push the circular door open and enter a brightly lit room. Your palms sweat. What's that sitting in the middle of the room? Oh, no! *A dentist's chair!*

"A sweets lover like you must have hundreds of cavities!" Billington growls.

No! You hate having your teeth examined. Even worse, you're pretty sure Billington isn't a trained dentist.

Which means you are in for a world of pain.

"I'll make you a deal," Billington offers. "If you don't have any cavities, I'll give you ten bags *full* of candy! And I'll let you go. Just sit in the chair!"

You don't want to spend any more time with this nut! Your first instinct is to make a run for it. But what if you don't make it? Billington *is* pretty fast. And he's standing right next to you.

Hmmm. Maybe you should stay. You brush every day. And your teeth feel fine. You don't think you have any cavities. If you pass Billington's test, he'll let you go!

"Will you accept my deal?" Billington asks.

Well, what do you say?

If you run for it, go to PAGE 61.

If you try your luck in the chair, go to PAGE 127.

You reach into your bag and grab the lollipop.

"Here!" you cry. "Take it! Now help me! Please!"

Outside, you hear the pirate's fists pound on the door. "I know you're in there, me hearty! Open up!"

Your heart is racing. A bloodthirsty pirate behind you! Vampires in front of you!

One of the vampires grabs you roughly. With inhuman strength he picks you up and slams you into the empty coffin!

"You want to live?" he asks. "Lie down in there!"

Lie down? In a coffin? That's for dead people!

The pirate bangs his body against the door. Once ... twice ...

A few more tries and he'll break it down!

"Don't be a fool," the other vampire says with a grin that exposes his fangs. "Lie down!"

Sorry! No other choice! Lie down in the coffin on PAGE 103.

You have exactly four seconds to do something before you're supper. You glance at the control panel of the car and see the problem: The car is in neutral!

You slam it in gear and step on the gas.

The tires squeal. You peel out, leaving skid marks behind you!

The Thing dives for you — but misses! You cruise off the bumper car platform, toward the other side of the room.

You zig and zag past the Ping-Pong tables and the video games. Your knuckles are white on the steering wheel. Your right foot is pressed so hard on the accelerator that it hurts.

But it's not enough to outrun the horrible ten-foot monster. You look over your shoulder and see that he's right behind you. . . .

And gaining!

You turn to see where you're going. Oh, no!

You're going to smash head-on into the wall!

Go to PAGE 102.

BOOM! BOOM! The sauna door shakes.

The monster howls in agony. Yes! The bolt is holding him! He crashes against the walls. Again. And again. But soon his howls and crashes become weaker. You hear a sigh and, finally, a whimper.

And then nothing at all. You peek through the glass window on the door. You see a large puddle!

Wow! The Thing has sweated away to nothing! You're not going to be eaten.

But you have one more problem to take care of.

Take care of it on PAGE 113.

For the first time in your life you're happy that your mother forced you to take those piano lessons!

You dash to the piano. You'll play the piece you learned for your piano recital, you decide.

Your body is shaking and your fingers are trembling, but somehow you remember the piece note for note!

The Thing stands there. Watching.

You can hear him panting. You can smell his hideous breath. You gulp as you think each note you play could be your last!

Only after you've played for a minute do you glance up at him. . . .

To your surprise, all the fierceness has drained out of the Thing's eyes. He looks — calm! He sways back and forth on the balls of his feet.

Yes! He's actually enjoying the music!

You near the end of the piece. You can't believe it worked! The last note sounds.

"ROOOOAR!" The Thing lets out a bellow — and swipes his massive paw down toward your shoulder blade!

Go on to PAGE 87.

You gasp.

The Thing swats you into the air!

This is it! The end!

You feel yourself land, but not on the hard floor. The Thing has caught you. He sets you down ... and then something weird happens ...

He puts out his paws on your shoulder ... and begins to dance!

The Thing closes his eyes, as if he's remembering your piano-playing. He purrs as he whisks you around the room, moving this way and that, to the imaginary beat.

Weird. But you'd sure rather be the Thing's dancing partner than his supper!

When your dance is over, the Thing bows low. Then he walks you to the kitchen and fills your bag up with sweets!

"What's going on?" a voice cries. It's Nathan.

"What are you doing?" he says to the Thing. "You're supposed to eat him, not give him my candy!"

Uh-oh. Trouble. Turn to PAGE 97.

So you hand over your trick-or-treat bag, which is sitting at your side.

"Dig in," you say, happy to give your candy away for a chance to get out of this weird place!

A satisfied smile spreads across the gorilla's face. He wipes a tear from his eye.

"Thank you," he mumbles. "No one ever gave me candy before!"

Wow! This ape is *nice*!

He stares happily into the bag for a second, then sticks his face inside and takes a deep whiff.

"All right," he says. "A deal's a deal."

He leads you out the door, down the hall, and past the lab to an elevator. He presses a button for you and bids you good-bye. When the doors finally open, directly before you is the red cobblestone path. Leading to the white mansion!

Maybe someone there can help you get out of Sunshine Court!

Hurry on to PAGE 108.

You lay your letters down. R-E-A-T. "Treat!" you declare!

"Excellent job!" your mother cries.

"Well done," your dad agrees, slapping you on your back.

Your sister smiles, and Champion yaps happily. You feel extremely happy — as though you've passed some sort of major test. Apparently, your parents agree.

"Well," your mom says. "I guess we can let you do a little more trick-or-treating."

"Really?" you say.

"Sure thing, sport," Dad replies with a cheerful nod.

You don't wait for them to change their minds. You're out the door in three seconds. Actually, you're happy to get away from them. There's no way that was your real family.

Now, if you want to try to get out of this place, all you've got to do is pick another house!

To visit the red house, go to PAGE 100.
To visit the orange house, go to PAGE 63.
To visit the yellow house, go to PAGE 40.
To visit the green house, go to PAGE 120.

The only other thing you have in your bag is the yellow rose you picked for your mom. It's a little crushed, but it's worth a try. You hold it out to the monster.

"S-s-see the pretty flower?" you stammer.

The monster lurches your way.

"The flower!" you cry. "Would you like it?"

The Thing wrinkles his brow . . . and blushes! Then he gently accepts the flower and takes a long whiff.

"Ahhhhh!" he moans happily. He sniffs deeply again, and stares at the rose. He seems entranced by it!

This is your chance! You climb out of the pool and run for your life toward the elevator.

Smart move. Because just as the elevator doors open, you turn to see the Thing toss the flower aside and scowl.

He gallops straight toward you! Hurry up and press a button!

To go to the basement to the gym, go to PAGE 94.

To go to the game room on the third floor, go to PAGE 5.

You run for the square door. Billington shuts it behind the two of you.

The first thing that hits you is the wonderful aroma. It's the one you smelled outside.

"I love my kitchen!" Billington announces. He suddenly seems like his original, bubbly self.

Pots and pans simmer on three huge stoves. The counter is covered with flour, brown sugar, and spices. Billington skips to one of the stoves and gives something a stir.

"This is going to be delicious!" he cries. "It's my chocolate-covered mocha supreme!" He cracks open an oven. "And this is where I'm cooking my pumpkin pie! All I need is my special ingredient, and everything will be ready."

Yum! Sounds like you're just in time! "Can I try some?" you ask.

Captain Billington turns around. He seems confused. "Try some?" he says. He wrinkles his brow. "That's impossible!"

"Why?" you ask.

Billington raises his eyebrows. "Because, dear child, you're going to be *in* it. You're my special ingredient!"

Yikes! Run or get cooked on PAGE 70.

Caught you!

You've seen a lot of things in this crazy Halloween adventure, but you never picked up a length of rope.

What did you think you were going to do? Fool us in our own book? No way.

You turn and face the monster. *CHOMP!* He devours you in one bite.

Too bad! But that's what you get for cheating in . . .

THE END.

You'll try the punch, as long as these elves leave you alone! You drain the glass, then glance around the party.

The dance floor is a sea of movement. People seem to be having fun, but you're eager to go trick-or-treating.

Someone taps your shoulder. A shriveled goblin stands at your side. Its face is covered with warts, its skin is light green, and its ears flop over like a dog's. Gross.

"Want to dance?" the goblin asks.

"Gee," you stammer. "I'd like to, but . . ."

"Get away!" A ghost floats over to the goblin. "I've always wanted to dance with a vampire!" it proclaims.

The ghost hovers in front of you — about two feet off the ground! Yikes! You swallow hard. That's either a real ghost or the best costume *you've* ever seen!

Either way, it's totally time to go. You take a step toward the door.

But the goblin grabs your wrists, and the ghost wraps itself around your legs. You can't move!

Looks like you're going to have to dance with one of them. Choose!

If you dance with the goblin, go to PAGE 96.
If you dance with the ghost, go to PAGE 25.

The elevator drops — all the way down to the basement.

You barrel through a set of swinging doors into the gym. Before you is an empty weight room.

You glance left and right, desperately looking for a place to hide.

"ROOOOOAAAARRRR!"

The Thing! He's tracked you to the basement . . . *already!*

You dive through a door on the far end of the room. You shut it behind you and bolt it. Whew!

You glance around. You're in the locker room.

Hide! your mind screams. Hide!

There's a row of shower stalls in front of you. Maybe you can hide there. No! you decide. Too obvious!

You glance over your shoulder. There are two other doors. One leads to the hot, dry sauna. The other to the wet, foggy steam room.

A creaking sound meets your ears. You glance back. No! The Thing is coming through the locker room door!

You have to hide! Now!

If you hide in the sauna, go to PAGE 57.
If you hide in the steam room, go to PAGE 52.

Faster and faster you spin. Your mouth is as dry as a desert. You're dizzy. Heat blasts you!

You bang on the door, but it's shut tight.

You try to yell — but your mouth is too dry....

It's getting hotter and hotter.

And you get dizzier . . .

And dizzier . . .

And dizzier . . .

Until . . .

Nothing.

Wow! Death by dryer!

It sure is hard to put a positive *spin* on this ending!

THE END

You swallow and grab the goblin's hand. "Let's boogie," you say bravely.

Ugh! Its hand is slimy. Eeew. It is *sooo* gross.

"Uh, nice mask," you comment.

"What mask?" the goblin asks. You chuckle, but the goblin doesn't laugh at all. It seems totally serious. But that can't be. That face has to be a mask. Doesn't it?

Finally the song ends. You are out of here!

You try to move away. What's this? The goblin's grip on your hand tightens. It puckers its lips at you.

Oh, no! It wants a kiss!

"Yeeech!" you yell. You've got to get out of this crazy party! Across the room you spot an open window. You run at it and dive through headfirst.

WHAM! You hit the ground. You're back in the middle of Sunshine Court.

Whew! Goblin kissing! You shudder at the thought. That red house was totally weird. And you only got one piece of candy in it! Better pick another house.

To go to the blue house, turn to PAGE 9.
To go to the orange house, turn to PAGE 63.
To go to the yellow house, turn to PAGE 40.
To go to the green house, turn to PAGE 120.

"RROOAR!" The Thing swats Nathan across the room, slamming him into the pantry door.

All right! Your music-playing put the monster on your side!

"Give me the key to the gate, Nathan!" you demand. "I'm out of here!"

With the monster on your side, Nathan can't exactly refuse. "No fair!" he whines, handing you the key.

You smile and pick up your bag of candy. Then the monster walks with you to the front door.

"Bye!" You wave to the Thing as you head outside.

But instead of staying put, the Thing follows you!

Cool, you think. A monster for a friend. With him around you're sure to *scare* up a lot more Halloween candy this year!

THE END

Your mind begins to race. Yeah, you've read enough *Goosebumps* books to know this whole setup is *bad* news!

Your family picked up and moved so fast. And everyone's being so nice! What if these people aren't really your parents and sister at all? What if they're aliens who have come to Earth to kill you?

Maybe you should go down to the living room and spy on your family. Then again, maybe you're safer in bed!

If you sneak to the living room, go to PAGE 66.
If you try to sleep, go to PAGE 117.

What a drag! English homework! On Halloween! Who can think about grammar and sentences when the rest of your friends are collecting mountains of candy? Life is *so* unfair. And what's up with your family? Why are they acting so incredibly weird?

Your bedroom door opens. You wheel around to find . . .

Your father! Wearing a vampire costume!

"Allow me to introduce myself," he says. His voice is suddenly deep and frightening. "I am a vampire, and I have come to suck your blood!"

"Hey, Dad," you say with a laugh. "That's my line!"

Your father grins. "But it's not just a line," he says. "It happens to be true! I'm not really your father. I'm a vampire!"

"No," you say. "It can't be!" But you know it's true. That's why your family's been acting so weird. They're probably *all* vampires!

The vampire "dad" swoops down at you. You scream and get up to run. But the monster is too fast for you.

"I told you you'd pay the consequences," he growls.

Boy, this Halloween turned out to be a big pain in the neck!

THE END

100

That red house looks nice, you decide. You jog up to it, then ring the bell. The door swings open and standing before you is . . .

Santa Claus?

"Ho, ho, ho!" he bellows. "Merry Christmas!"

Christmas? This guy needs some serious holiday help.

"Uh, yeah," you say. "Merry Christmas to you too."

A tall woman dressed as a werewolf appears at Santa's side. "We need more punch," she squawks.

"More punch?" Santa echoes. He laughs. "And the party's just beginning!"

Your eyes go wide. Ohhhh! It's a costume party.

As the werewolf retreats into the house, you see Santa reach into his red sack. When he faces you again he's holding a piece of red licorice and a mango lollipop in one hand, and a shiny red apple in the other.

"Take one!" he commands. "Then come join the fun!"

Put either the licorice, the lollipop, or the apple in your bag and join the party on PAGE 69. (Don't forget to write down what you took!)

It's your classmate *Nathan Rickles*!

"Nathan?" you exclaim. "What are you doing here?"

Nathan smiles. "This is where I live. I'd like to show you around. There's lots to see. Tons to do!"

You can't believe it! You're saved!

You think of your buddies on Pearl Street. Once Nathan lets you out, you may still be able to catch them. If you run the whole way.

"Dude," you say to Nathan. "This is one weird place you live in. I'd like to hang out and talk about it, but maybe some other time. Right now, could you just let me out of here?"

"So soon?" Nathan says, adjusting his glasses. "Stick around! My dad's out of town and the butler just gave me the key to the back kitchen — where we keep all the candy."

Nathan dangles a key in front of your face. You remember the giant bag of sweets he showed you earlier in the evening, including that Double-Chocolate-Triple-Caramel Delight bar!

True, you're eager to catch up with your friends. But the thought of all that candy is too big a temptation.

"All right," you say. "Let's hit the candy stash."

Follow Nathan to PAGE 29.

SCCCREEEEECHHHHHH!

You turn the steering wheel with all your might.

The car spins out. When you skid to a halt, you find yourself facing the opposite direction. You put the pedal to the metal and . . .

Shoot through the monster's legs!

"ARRRRGGGHHH!" he cries and turns to give chase.

But the monster is so twisted up he stumbles. Yes! A few more valuable seconds!

You thunder out of the room. You barrel down the hallway and slam on the brakes by the elevator.

SCREEECHHHHHH!

You jump out of the car and press the elevator button. You press again. Where is it? You don't have time to wait!

Maybe you should take the stairs instead.

Better decide and be quick about it!

To take the elevator, go to PAGE 76.
To take the stairs, go to PAGE 110.

SLAM! The coffin door shuts on top of you. It's pitch-black inside!

You hear the pirate crash through the door. "Where's the little one?" he yells.

"The kid went out the back," one vampire replies.

Incredible, you think! The vampires covered for you!

You hear the heavy steps of the pirate as he races out the back door.

"Okay, open up," you call, rapping on the coffin lid.

But you don't hear a sound. You feel a twinge of panic and pound the top of the coffin again.

"It's hot in here!" you cry. "Open up!"

Still nothing! What's going on? Are the vampires going to leave you here?

The bottom of the coffin drops out from under you!

"Aaaah!" You're careening down a slide. Then you shoot out into the air.

FROMP! You land in the middle of a pile of pillows. What just happened? You shake your head and look around.

Yes! In front of you is a cobblestone path. And it's leading to the white mansion! Maybe there's someone in there who can help you get out of this freaky place.

Go on to PAGE 108.

104

SPLASH!

You dive into the deep end of the pool. . . .

Just as the Thing leaps into the room! He rushes to the edge of the water.

Then he paws the ground, breathing heavily through his flaring nostrils. The Thing swipes his paw at you from the side of the pool.

Yes! You realize. You were right! He *can't* swim!

The Thing stands on his hind legs. He lets loose an earsplitting howl of frustration.

"Too bad, Thing!" you call. "All I have to do is tread water for an hour. Then I'm home free!"

"He-he-he." You hear a nerdy giggle from the side of the pool. You turn. Nathan!

A low whooshing sound meets your ears . . . gradually it grows louder and louder.

Oh, no! There's a small whirlpool in the middle of the water. You gasp as you realize what's happening.

Nathan is draining all the water out of the pool!

"Nathan, please don't!" you plead.

But he just cackles and runs from the room. What will you do now?

Tread water on PAGE 38.

You decide to push the lever. The operating table begins to spin ... and spin ... and spin — faster and faster — until you are thrown free. Yes! You made it!

You run down a hallway and see a yellow door. You push it open. *SLAM!* It shuts behind you.

Whew! That was close. You catch your breath, then take in the scene in front of you. In the center of the room is a giant metal contraption, covered with colored buttons.

Dr. Hillenthrobben's voice fills the room from a loudspeaker: "I see you found my experiment after all. I'm creating the perfect candy and need you to help me! Eat, child! Eat!"

Eat what? you think. There's no candy here.

The machine starts to rumble. Then it belches black smoke. You gasp. Then there's a terrifying *BANG!* You drop to your knees, shaking. The machine is going to blow!

A thin line of purple smoke comes out of the smokestack. And ...

A tasty array of candy travels down a conveyer belt! You can't believe it.

"Eat!" Hillenthrobben cries. "Eat!"

Like he has to tell you twice? Get to it on PAGE 43.

"Another one of my inventions," Nathan explains.

Then you feel yourself lifted in the air. You hear a loud *BANG*. A bright light burns your eyes.

Hey! Where are you? Hold on a second! You find yourself standing next to Nathan! And the knight in shining armor from the picture you were just looking at!

Somehow Nathan has pulled you into the book with him!

Go on to PAGE 128.

You pull the lever. The table begins to shake. Then . . .

Whoooah! The table you're lying on plunges through a hole in the floor! Above, you see Dr. Hillenthrobben peering down at you, his face growing smaller and smaller.

WHAM! You touch down in a hall lined with mirrors.

Soon the hall forks off in two directions. You have to choose which way to go. Oh, man! This is some kind of mirror maze. You hate mazes!

You pause for a moment — which way do you go?

What's that? Footsteps echoing in the hall — coming toward you. Who can that be? Only Hillenthrobben — or Samson! Trembling with fear, you turn and tear down the left hallway.

The footsteps grow louder!

You don't dare stop running. If you do, Dr. Hillenthrobben will drag you back to the lab! Then who knows what will happen?

You hear Hillenthrobben's voice: "Running is no use! I'll find you!"

You sprint toward a light at the end of the hall.

No! You've reached a dead end! Wait — not a dead end! On either side of you are there are two brass doors!

To take the door on the right, go to *PAGE 17*.
To take the door on the left, go to *PAGE 28*.

The white mansion rises up before you — your only hope of getting out of this place.

Except now that you're closer to it, you're not so sure you want to go in.

At close range, it looks a little — unfriendly.

But what choice do you have? The tall iron fence around Sunshine Court is locked. Maybe the people in the big white mansion have a key. You have to give it a try.

After everything that's just happened to you, your legs feel a bit weak with fear. But you walk up the cobblestone path to the front door and ring the bell.

Hurry on to PAGE 54.

You dash to the tree and get climbing. Better hurry, you think. Before the Thing shows up and sees you!

Up, up, up you go. At the top you pause to catch your breath.

Wow! What a view!

You're in the middle of an enormous forest. There are trees and more trees as far as the eye can see. What happened to the mansion? you think. What kind of place is this? And how are you going to get out of here?

What's that — in the distance? A thin gray line. It's smoke! Hey, maybe the smoke is coming from a village! From people who can help you get back home! Now, if you can just get there without the Thing catching you . . .

"Eeek! Eeek! Eeek!"

A monkey swings from a vine and lands on your head.

"Get away!" you shout.

But the monkey pushes you! You lose your balance. . . .

Ahhhhhhhh! You're falling fast toward the ground!

This is it! You close your eyes and wait to pound into the earth.

Go on to PAGE 8.

You take the stairs and rush to the top floor.

You push open a door. You find yourself in a large oak room lined with shelves of old, musty books.

The library, you realize.

You run down the aisles, breathing heavily, heart pounding. You're desperate to find a hiding place. Nothing looks any good. But you're beginning to relax. For the first time since Nathan's little "game" began, you don't hear the Thing.

Maybe you've actually lost him, you think. Maybe all you have to do is to find a good book, sit in the corner, and read till your hour is up.

But then you hear something move around the corner. Your blood goes cold. You feel weak with fear.

Could the Thing have followed you up here so fast?

Do you dare peek around the corner to find out?

Yes, you do on PAGE 47.

You blink. Yup. The snow is still there. You didn't imagine it at all.

This is too weird for you. You turn to walk back out the door you used a moment ago.

Hey! It's not there! Instead, you see more snow, stretching for miles and miles!

You have no idea how this could be happening, but one thing is for sure. You are in huge trouble. Unless you can find a way out of this mess. But where? How?

The footsteps! The ones you came into this place to investigate. You hear them again! Coming toward you! Maybe it's someone who can help.

You trudge forward. And gasp when you see what's making the sound! A gigantic polar bear! Headed straight for you!

Shiver on to PAGE 81.

112

With the Thing hot on your tracks, you dash across the room. You grab the guitar and strum a chord, ready to play the way your music teacher taught you.

The Thing stops short. He wrinkles his brow.

"Please let this work," you whisper. It's your only chance. The Thing grunts. He motions for you to continue.

Yes! It is working! You jam on the guitar. The Thing seems to like rock and roll. Most important, he isn't killing you.

You bend your knees. You wiggle your hips. Now it looks like the Thing is smiling! Then something even better happens: He begins to clap!

Yes! You're safe!

BOOOIINNNNGGGG!

You look down at the guitar. . . .

Noooo! you wail.

Two of the strings have snapped!

How are you supposed to make music now?

Get out of this one on PAGE 73.

You take the elevator to the first floor and find Nathan standing there, by the front door.

"Wh-what? You're still alive?" Nathan stutters.

You grab him by the shoulders. "Give me the key to the gate!" you demand.

Nathan remains silent. You grab the back of his pants. "Give me the key or I'll give you the biggest wedgie you've ever had in your life!"

"Nooo," Nathan moans. "Not a wedgie!" He reaches into his pocket and pulls out a big black key.

You grab it from him, then throw him in a closet. You lock him inside. His father will be home soon. Let him explain what happened to the gym. He'll be grounded forever!

As for you, you walk out into the cool night.

You unlock Sunshine Court's heavy iron gate, and you are out of there! You run all the way to Pearl Street. After all, you've still got time to meet your friends for, not the end, but . . .

**THE BEGINNING OF YOUR MOST
FABULOUS HALLOWEEN!**

114

You stumble into the room. The elf hits the light.

"Tada!" he cries.

You blink in the bright light. When you can see again, you gasp. You're standing in a large room filled with . . .

What's it filled with? What? Find out on PAGE 27.

You don't want to hurt anyone! You leave the skewer where it is and dash for the door. But Billington is too quick.

He slams it shut.

Uh-oh. No escape!

You take a step back. . . .

Your entire body shakes with fear.

The madman merely laughs and squeezes your arm.

"Excellent!" he coos. "You're quite tender!"

He lumbers across the room and opens the oven.

And throws you in!

Sweat it out on PAGE 15.

116

You creep into the heart-shaped cave.

Out of the wind! Ahhh! Your toes begin to tingle and come back to life. You crawl forward until the cave opens up to the size of a small room.

Yikes! The room! It's lined with skeletons! *Human* skeletons! You notice one of them holds a beat-up notebook in its bony hand. You take the notebook and open it.

"The Diary of an Arctic Explorer," you begin reading. A few more lines tell you that standing before you are the bones of six explorers who died in the cold!

Oh, no. The awful truth sinks in. That means you might die too! Then you notice something. In the hands of another explorer is a map. You grab it and spread it out on a rock.

Lucky you! It's a map to where they stashed their sled! You could take the map, find the sled, and ride it all the way home!

You run for the mouth of the cave. Then you stop! Then again, maybe you'd be smarter to wait for the polar bear to return for you!

If you put the map in your trick-or-treat bag, go to PAGE 16. (And don't forget to write it down on your pad.)

If you wait for the polar bear, go to PAGE 49.

There's no such thing as aliens, you tell yourself. You just have an overactive imagination. You roll over, determined to get some sleep.

Then you hear it. A strange scraping sound.

Nervous, you reach out and switch on the light. But the room is still. All appears to be well. You take a deep breath and tell yourself to relax one more time. You turn the light back off. . . .

There's the scraping noise again!

And then you sit bolt upright and turn the lights back on. At first you think you're seeing things. But then it becomes clear that you aren't.

Because the walls are closing in!

Closing in on you!

BANG! The moving walls knock down your desk!

BOOM! Your dresser crashes to the floor!

In another minute you're going to be a wall sandwich!

Find out if you escape on PAGE 124.

Nathan flicks on the lights.

You're in a lab — an enormous room filled with strange gadgets, smoking potions, and frothing test tubes.

And in the back . . .

In a cage . . .

Is something positively hideous! He's a giant monster, half-lion (you think), and half-human. He is covered with thick, bristly fur. He has giant yellow eyes. And teeth that make Jaws look like a wimp. He roars again.

"Meet the Thing!" Nathan yells over the noise. He pushes you toward the center of the room. "I made him in my spare time!"

"You *made* him?" you ask, beginning to shake.

"That's right," Nathan says. "He's ten feet tall. He weighs five hundred pounds. And boy, oh, boy, does he love to eat!"

"R-r-really?" you stammer as the Thing roars again.

"Really!" Nathan declares. "And there's something else about the Thing that you need to know. Something very important."

Find out what on PAGE 21.

You ring the bell...one, two, three times. Hmmm. No answer. On instinct, you give the door a little push.

CRRREEEAKKK! The door opens. From inside the house a stale breeze blows in your face. You peek inside.

"Anybody home?" you stutter.

Whoa! This looks nothing like that happy, sunny place you expected from the outside. In fact, it totally looks like a haunted house! The kind you went to at the county fair last summer! Cool!

You take a few steps inside.

Cobwebs dance overhead. Bats fly through the rafters. And a skeleton dangles against the opposite wall, smiling hideously. You feel something scamper across your feet. You glance down. A rat! A real rat! You bite your lip to keep from screaming.

CLOMP! CLOMP! What's that sound? *Footsteps?*

You want to know where they're coming from, but do you have the guts to check them out?

If you forget the footsteps and leave, go to PAGE 11.

If you check out the footsteps, go to PAGE 33.

You stand on the red cobblestone path and look up at the green house. A chimney sticks out of its roof. And out of the chimney twists a thin line of purple smoke.

Whoa!

Purple smoke?

You lift your nose and take a whiff. You can't tell what's cooking, but it sure smells great. You have a strong feeling you're going to score lots of candy here!

With your trick-or-treat bag at the ready, you jog the few remaining steps to the front door and lean on the bell.

The door swings open, revealing a tall man in a purple jumpsuit. He has a closely cropped red beard and bright green eyes.

"Well, well, well!" he shouts, suddenly pumping your hand up and down. "So glad to see you! Thrilled you dropped by! What a lovely costume! I love vampires! Used to want to be a vampire myself, but I hate working nights! Ha ha! What took you so long? No matter! You're just in time! Come in!"

Uh — okay. Follow the man inside to PAGE 45.

The mirror is closest. You grasp it in your hand.

The Thing stomps forward. You swing at him with the mirror.

"Get away!" you screech. "Keep away!"

The Thing continues toward you. You're doomed! You shove the mirror toward him and squeeze your eyes shut.

"Aaaaaaaaaahhh!"

Wait a minute. That's not you screaming. It's the Thing! You open your eyes.

Wow! The Thing has caught sight of himself in the mirror. He's shrieking from looking at his own reflection!

As you stare at him, the Thing freezes in place. He takes on a grayish tone. The screaming stops.

After a moment, you cautiously approach the Thing. You touch his shoulder, and gasp.

The Thing has turned to stone! Which means you're free to go!

But not before you give Nathan Rickles a piece of your mind — and grab a few of his candy bars on the way out.

Which makes this ending one of the sweetest in the whole book!

THE END

You crawl on your belly through the dirt tunnel. Soon a light grows in the distance.

Yes! you think when you reach the end. You're free! You're outside again! Hey, and there's that guy in the Santa suit you saw at the party! What's that he's sitting in? A sleigh? With eight tiny reindeer?

You've hit the jackpot! Christmas has come early! "Santa" and his sleigh can get you out of here!

As if he read your mind, Santa reaches out and grabs you! He lifts you high into the air and places you atop the sleigh. "You're coming with me, kid!" Santa commands.

Then he turns to the reindeer. "Yaaaaaa!"

The reindeer barrel down the backyard, then lift off into the air!

The air?

Wait a minute. Reindeer can't fly. Unless, somehow, you've managed to find the *real* Santa!

Ride on to PAGE 18.

The Thing roars again. You tear for the door. You throw it open and barrel down the hall as fast as you can.

You reach the elevator and press the button again and again. Where is the stupid thing?

Nathan's crazy giggling echoes down the hall after you. No wonder he told you to come to the white mansion! He lured you here! He wants the Thing to kill you!

DING! The elevator doors open and you jump in. But where should you go? Luckily, there's a floor plan of the mansion taped to the elevator wall.

"Sixty! Ready or not, here Thing comes!" you hear Nathan shout.

Yikes! Press a button, quick!

To go to the gym in the basement, turn to PAGE 94.

To go to the music room on the first floor, turn to PAGE 59.

To go to the pool on the second floor, turn to PAGE 41.

To go to the game room on the third floor, turn to PAGE 5.

Desperate, you stand on your bed and look around for an escape. Near the ceiling is a tiny window that leads to the roof: your only hope! But how do you reach that high?

Then it hits you. You'll use your bed like a trampoline!

You jump once, twice, three times into the air! You stretch. . . .

And grab the windowsill with your fingertips!

CRRRRUNNNNCCHHHHH! The bed is crushed between the walls. You have to get out of here! You pull yourself up onto the windowsill, then roll onto the roof.

OOF! You fling yourself onto the ground.

You lie still for a moment, making sure you're still in one piece. Then you slowly sit up.

It takes you a while to get your bearings, but soon enough you see that you are back in Sunshine Court!

Turn to PAGE 134.

"Arrrggggh!" You fall to the ground, struggling against Champion. The dog seems to have super-strength!

You gaze up, Your mom standing above you. You're about to ask for her help, when her eyes glow a sickly green.

"Stupid human," she growls. "I told you I'd make you suffer!"

Human? This thing standing above you isn't your mom at all! It's some kind of monster!

You should have known. She was acting so weird.

Well, you made a big mistake — and now Champion is going to make sure you really suffer for it.

THE END

You look around. Where *is* that bag of candy? Oh, no! You must have left it in the lab!

"Sorry," you say. "But I don't have my candy."

Samson drops to his knees and clenches his hairy hands. Hot tears pour out of his eyes.

"No candy?" he cries. He pounds the floor with his fists. The tremors he causes shake your entire body. "I want candy!"

Your edge toward the door. Samson seems a little too upset about not getting any candy. You hope he won't take out his disappointment on you.

"W-w-well," you stammer. "If you lead me out, I could get some more candy and bring it back to you."

"Candy!" Samson bellows. "Now!"

He rises to his full height. He pounds his chest and takes a step toward you! Uh-oh!

"Wait!" you cry. "There has to be a way to . . ."

Before you can finish, Samson lifts you up over his head. He opens a hidden door on the other side of the room.

"No!" you yell. "Noooooo!"

Samson throws you through the doorway into the darkness!

Find out where you are on PAGE 58.

Best to go along with Billington, you decide. You don't want to make him angry. And maybe he isn't as bad a dentist as he looks.

You take a seat in the chair. Please, please, please, you beg silently. Just look at my teeth quickly and let me go.

Billington gazes into your mouth. "Four cavities!" he exclaims. "No candy for you!"

Your heart drops. Billington turns and reaches for a shelf. What's he searching for?

WHHHHHHHHIRRRRRRRRRRR! A terrible noise meets your ears. No! It's a drill!

"Four cavities to fill!" he cries.

He steps toward you. Your chest heaves. You're so scared you can't get air. Then you see something. A gas mask! And it's just within your reach!

Hurry up! Grab it and defend yourself!

Take the gas mask and go to PAGE 7.

128

You wheel around. Yup. You're in the middle of a large field. Just like the one in the book you were holding.

"How did you do this?" you stammer.

Nathan giggles madly.

"Is this the knave who is going to help me slay the dreaded beast?" the knight asks Nathan. He points to you.

"His name is Thing, not Beast," Nathan corrects the knight. "And, yes, this is the knave!"

Nathan giggles some more.

"Excellent!" the knight says. "Come, then!"

Your legs go weak. Somehow, Nathan has transported the Thing here too. To kill you.

"Of course, you don't have to battle the Thing," Nathan tells you.

Huh? You stop.

"You can come with me! I'm going to the arena to see the jousting exhibition!" Nathan gives you a wicked smile.

Being a spectator at a jousting exhibition sure *sounds* better than fighting the Thing. But you don't like the smile on Nathan's face. He may have something tricky up his sleeve. Which should you choose?

If you go with the knight, turn to PAGE 50.
If you go with Nathan, turn to PAGE 67.

The knight hands you a lance. "Take your best shot," he instructs you.

Shaking in fear, you raise the lance. You take aim — and throw.

You hit the Thing right between the eyes!

Yes! The monster moans and hits the ground!

A swarm of villagers runs up the mountain. They lift you onto their shoulders and carry you into the knight's castle. A banquet is thrown in your honor. You're a hero!

That night you go to sleep on a giant bed at the knight's place. You've never been so tired. That's when you start to dream. . . .

What in the world? You wheel around, panicked. Could it be? You're suddenly back in the white mansion. On the first floor!

"*ROOOOAAAARRRR!*"

Oh, no! Back with the Thing!

Is this a nightmare? Or reality? You're not sure.

Oh, well. While you try to figure it out, we're going trick-or-treating! So, for us, this is . . .

**THE VERY BEST END
IN THE WHOLE BOOK!**

130

Your jaw drops. Your eyes go wide.

You're in a room *filled* with candy!

Not just a little candy. Not even a lot of candy. But tons of candy. *Mountains* of it.

Yes! You hit the jackpot. The grand prize!

Boy, Nathan sure knew what he was talking about.

"Take all you want!" Captain Billington cries. "As much as you can carry! And start eating too!"

You don't need to be told twice. You shove ten, fifteen, twenty candy bars in your bag. (Be sure to write them down.) Plus, you scarf down a few right there and then.

Your buddies will be so jealous, you think. You'll be the envy of your class!

"Thank you," you gush. "This was amazing!"

Captain Billington salutes. "Think nothing of it!"

You turn to go out the door. But Captain Billington's hand grabs your shoulder. He turns you back around.

"I don't recall giving you permission to leave, sailor!" he snaps at you.

Uh-oh. Is the captain losing it? Find out on PAGE 39.

You're in enough hot water as it is. You're not about to make things worse by taking the advice of a thief!

"Don't trust me, eh?" Gildenblithen says with a scowl. "Fine." He lurches toward you.

"Wait," you stammer, backing up. "It's not that I don't trust you. It's . . ."

Gildenblithen reaches into his pocket and takes out — a whistle?

He blows it with all his might: *SCREEEE-EECCCHHHHHH!*

"You called?" someone asks from the doorway. Dr. Hillenthrobben!

"I have the specimen," Gildenblithen says.

"Good work," Hillenthrobben replies. "Take the child back to the lab!"

Your heart pounds as you realize the truth: All this running around has been part of some hideous experiment!

"Samson!" Hillenthrobben cries. The gorilla stomps into the room. "Take the child back to the lab for the final phase," Hillenthrobben commands.

"Final phase?" Your voice shakes with terror.

"Yes," Hillenthrobben replies. "The part in which you sacrifice your life for the sake of science!"

Meet your fate on PAGE 68.

You dash into the music room and slam the door. You can only hope the Thing didn't see you!

You search for a place to hide. But — there's nowhere! The room is practically bare! Standing before you is a grand piano. In the corner is a guitar and a tuba.

CRASSSSHHHHHH!

You shriek as the door explodes. Shards of wood fly into the room. The Thing thunders in!

You're face-to-face with him! His eyes lock on yours.

You take a step back. The Thing licks his lips. His sharklike teeth glint in the overhead light. Then he moves toward you!

You close your eyes and get ready for the end.

But then you remember something . . . a phrase your mother used to say when she sang your little sister to sleep: "Music soothes the savage beast."

That's it! You'll play music! It's your only chance! But which instrument should you play?

If you play the piano, go to PAGE 86.
If you play the guitar, go to PAGE 112.
If you play the tuba, go to PAGE 23.

You reach into your candy bag and pull out the apple. The pirate narrows his eyes. He licks his lips.

"Ahoy there! Is that what I think it is?"

With that sword still at your throat, you can barely manage a nod. But you do.

The pirate grabs the fruit with a filthy hand and shoves it into his mouth.

"I love me apples, me hearty!" he thunders. He eats the whole thing in one chomp.

Then he glares at you once again. His eyes are filled with pure hatred and evil.

"Now, to take care of *you*," he growls. He swings his sword down at you.

Yikes. Looks like you're going to be peeled and cored, just like an apple.

What a rotten Halloween trick!

THE END

You run to the iron entrance gate. Still locked. There's no way out — at least for the time being.

You glance at your feet. There's the red cobblestone path: leading straight to the orange house.

Go to PAGE 63.

Wait a minute. Did he just say "tomb"? No. It can't be. He must have said "room." You just misunderstood.

"Well, I'm out of here," the elf announces. He moves to the door.

"Hey! Wait for me!" You sprint for the door.

Too late.

SLAM! The elf has disappeared.

Leaving you stuck in this cold, damp room!

Get out on PAGE 46.

About the Author

R.L. Stine is the most popular author in America. He is the creator of the *Goosebumps*, *Give Yourself Goosebumps*, *Fear Street*, and *Ghosts of Fear Street* series, among other popular books. He has written over 250 scary novels for kids. Bob lives in New York City with his wife, Jane, teenage son, Matt, and dog, Nadine.